You are my Wish come True

By Marianne Richmond

You are my Wish come True

is dedicated to
Cole, Adam, Julia, and Will;
my four wishes-come-true. — MR

Library of Congress Control Number: 2007941518

Marianne Richmond Studios, Inc.
3900 Stinson Boulevard NE
Minneapolis, MN 55421
www.mariannerichmond.com

ISBN 10: 1-934082-60-0
ISBN 13: 978-1-934082-60-7

Illustrations by Marianne Richmond

Book design by Sara Dare Biscan

Printed by Cimarron
Minneapolis, MN, USA
Second Printing, December 2009

Also available from author & illustrator
Marianne Richmond:

The Gift of an Angel
The Gift of a Memory
Hooray for You!
The Gifts of Being Grand
I Love You So...
Dear Daughter
Dear Son
Dear Mom
Dear Granddaughter
Dear Grandson
My Shoes Take Me Where I Want to Go
Fish Kisses and Gorilla Hugs
Happy Birthday to You!
I Love You so Much...
I Wished for You, an adoption story
Big Brother
Big Sister

Beginner Boards for the youngest child
simply said... and *smartly said...* mini books
for all occasions

Please visit **www.mariannerichmond.com**

Home is
where
The
Love
is

Mama and Barley Bear snuggled in their favorite cuddle spot.

"*Mama,*" said Barley. "Tell me again how I'm your *wish come true.*"

Mama smiled. Barley loved to hear

about how he was Mama's special wish.

"A long time ago," said Mama to Barley,
"a wish started growing in my heart.
At first, it was a quiet wish
that nobody knew. Then it became
an out-loud wish that grew

and
grew and *grew*.

Until one day,
my wish
came true."

"**Me!**" said Barley.
"I was your
wish come true!"

"Yes," said Mama.
"<u>You</u> are
my
wish
come
true."

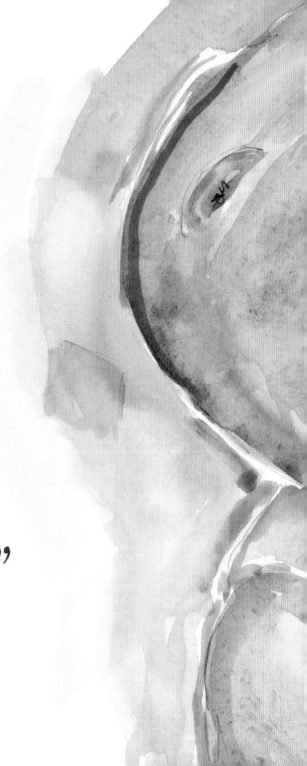

Barley wiggled to get more comfortable.

"Why did you wish for
me, Mama?" asked Barley.

Barley wished for things like a new comic book or

a pet lizard. He had never wished for a somebody.

"Because," explained Mama, "I had
an empty place in my heart that
I wanted to fill with love
for a special child like you.
Someone who would be
my cuddly little one, and
I would be his Mama."

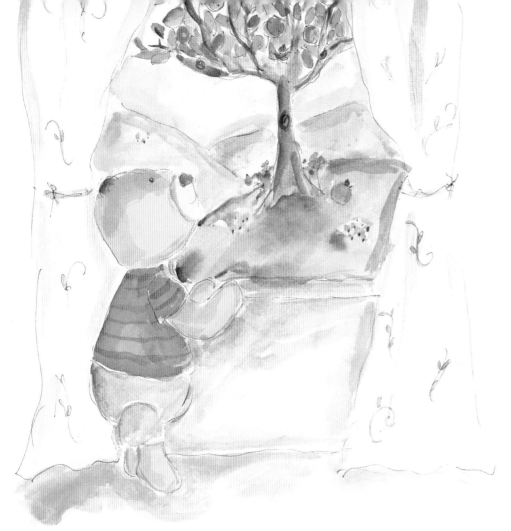

Barley got up and looked out the window that faced

the big apple tree out back.

"*Did* you wish for me all day, Mama?"
Barley asked. "Or only when the
stars were out?"

"**All** the time," said Mama, softly. "I wished for you with my morning coffee, and when I made my bed. I couldn't get my wish for you out from in my head."

That was a lot of wishing, thought Barley.

He thought of all the things he did at school like math and lunch and reading. He couldn't imagine wishing through all of them.

"Mama," said Barley,
his voice a whisper. "Did you wish for me
by name?"

He liked his name, he thought to himself.

Mama tilted her head to show

she was remembering.

"When I first wished
my wish," said Mama to Barley,
"I didn't know your name. Or
if you'd be a boy or girl. But that
didn't stop my wishing.
I asked God to think about my wish and
to create the child who would be
the perfect one for me."

"*Barley,*" said Mama, her eyes spilling over with tears. "*Of* all the children in the whole wide world, God made <u>you</u> for me."

This made Barley feel really special.

There are lots of children in the world,

he reminded himself. And God made him!

Mama patted her belly. "When I found out you were growing inside my tummy, I was excited and nervous all at the same time!"

Barley imagined himself curled up like a little ball in his Mama's tummy.

"I was really in there?" asked Barley, putting his hand on top of Mama's.

"Yes," smiled Mama. "As small as a pickle. But as you grew, my tummy grew bigger. You kicked and rolled. Sometimes," said Mama, "I thought you were doing somersaults in there!"

"I wanted to come out and see you," giggled Barley.

"Me, too," said Mama.

"Did you ever think," wondered Barley, "that your wish might not come true?"

"Oh yes..." said Mama, remembering how long the waiting seemed sometimes.

"I wished for you long before you started growing in my tummy... and through many trips to the doctor for check-ups.

I wished for you while I decorated your room and shopped for baby things...."

"**And,**" said Mama, "I wished for you through the wonderful parties for you and I."

Barley wondered why grown-ups would buy him presents

before he was even born.

How could they have known what he liked?

He had a hard enough time

picking out gifts for his friends.

Mama continued, "*I wished* and waited while I counted down the hundreds of days until I met you."

Barley wasn't good at waiting.

He wanted his birthday to be three times a year.

"During the waiting," said Mama,
    "I would imagine *you*."

"Imagine me?" repeated Barley.

"*Yes,*" said Mama.

"I imagined what you'd look like,
or what color your fur would be.
I imagined you in your room,
    playing with your blocks and trains.
I wondered, too, if you'd like
    soccer or piano or art projects."

"**Did** you imagine me to look exactly like I do?" _{asked Barley.}

"You, Barley, are more
beautiful than
I ever dreamed,"

said Mama.

Barley knew Mama was thinking about

the lucky part in her story,

because her eyes grew big and round.

"One day…" said Mama,

brightening as she spoke,

"One glorious, special, wonderful day,

I knew my wish

was about to come true."

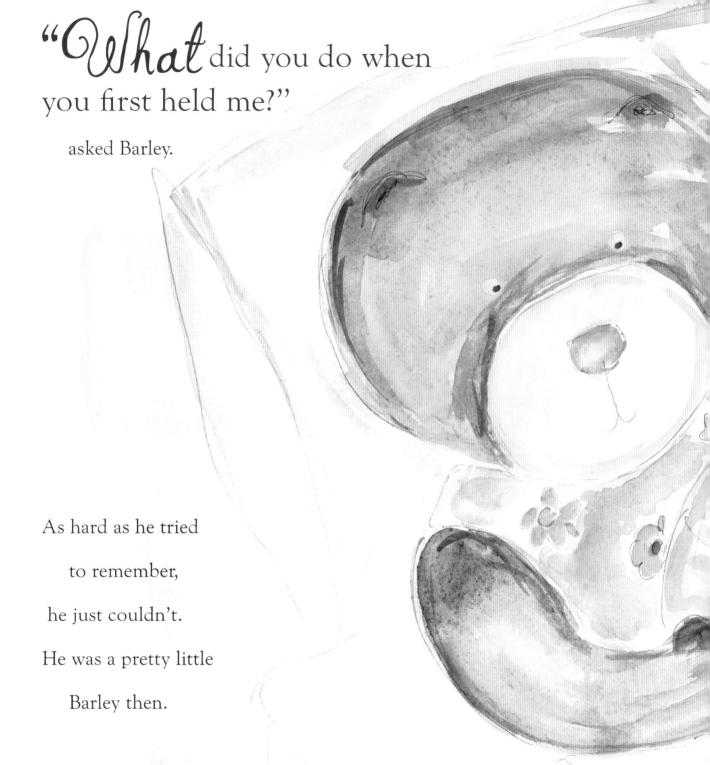

"**What** did you do when you first held me?"

asked Barley.

As hard as he tried

to remember,

he just couldn't.

He was a pretty little

Barley then.

"Oh, Barley,"
said Mama.
"I fell deeply
in love with you.
I looked into your
sweet face, and right
then, you became

my *wish*
come
true."

Barley felt cozy about what his Mama was telling him, but a thought niggled at him.

"Mama," said Barley. "Me and you are in the same family, but we don't look the same. You have dark fur, and I have light fur with brown ears. Is this okay?"

"*Yes,* Barley," she said. "Some families look alike, and others don't.

All families are different.

What makes a family is their *love* for each other."

That makes sense, thought Barley.

He liked Mama's answer.

He loved being part of her family.

'click'

"Do wishes *always* come true?"
asked Barley, thinking again

about the pet lizard he still wished for.

"No," said Mama. "Not all of our wishes come true. But don't ever stop wishing for the hopes of your heart."

"I won't," said Barley.

Maybe he'd ask for a goldfish instead.

"But *I* came true," said Barley, proudly.

"Yes, you did, Barley," said Mama.
"I wished for you, and you
are always and forever
my *wish*
come
true."

Mama and Barley stayed right there

in their cuddle spot, both thinking that

always and forever was a good amount of time.

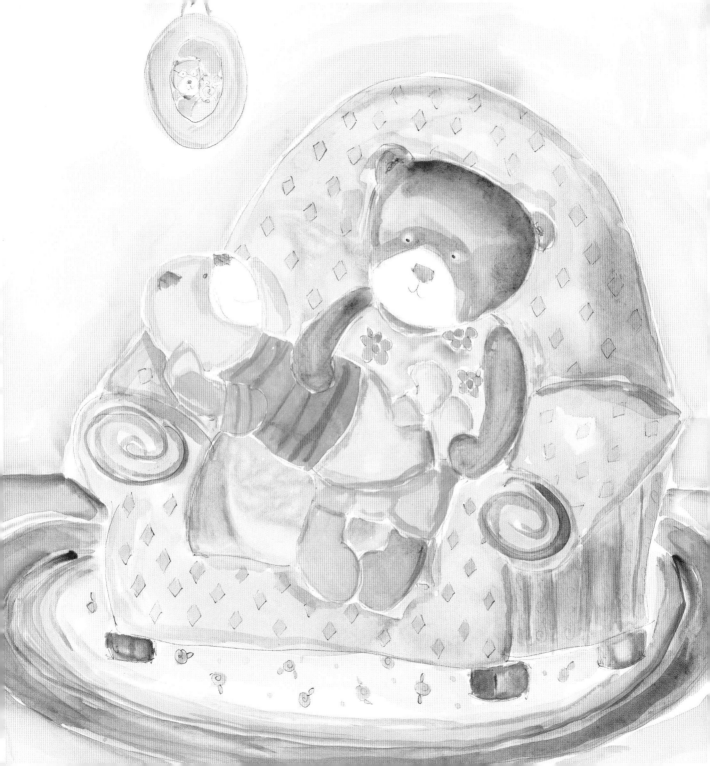

Bear Hugs Welcome Here,